THROUGH THE FIRE

From a distance, Rachel had been as excited as her brother Will by the gabled houses, the gleaming spires and palaces of London. But as the cart drew nearer to the noisy squalor of the city, her excitement turned to angry confusion at the cause of their coming.

Why had Father brought them to this evil place? Would they ever return to the peaceful beauty of Bledlow Green? What crime could their fellow Quakers have committed to justify their cruel imprisonment amongst murderers and thieves in King Charles's gaols?

With Rachel and Will's deeper understanding of the Quaker faith came a new courage – a courage which helped them to face not only the injustice of their father's own arrest, but the nightmare of being trapped inside Bridewell prison whilst the Great Fire of London burnt its way relentlessly towards them.

The author wishes to thank Elfrida Vipont for her advice and help concerning Quaker customs and history

Hester Burton
Through the Fire

Beaver Books

First published in 1969 by
Hamish Hamilton Limited
90 Great Russell Street, London WC1B 3PT

This paperback edition published in 1976 by
The Hamlyn Publishing Group Limited
London · New York · Sydney · Toronto
Astronaut House, Feltham, Middlesex, England

©Copyright Text Hester Burton 1969
©Copyright Illustrations Gareth Floyd 1969
ISBN 0 600 38739 9

Printed in England by
Cox & Wyman Limited, Reading
Set in Monotype Baskerville
Line drawings by Gareth Floyd
Cover illustration by Michael Jackson

Contents

For Elizabeth Gloyne – with love

Historical Note

THE QUAKERS George Fox founded the group of Christians called 'the Friends' in the middle of the seventeenth century. The Friends believe that God speaks to each of us in our hearts and that it is the duty of Christians to listen to what He says. For this purpose, Friends meet together in silence on Sundays (First Days) and speak only when they feel that God has moved them to tell others what is in their hearts. Sometimes in the early days – at the time in which the following story is set – Friends were so moved by their communion with God that they shook or 'quaked'. And so their enemies scornfully called them 'the Quakers'.

The Quakers were good and honest people but, at first, they were very unpopular in England. Neither the Puritans nor the members of the Church of England understood their new religion and each, when they were in power, persecuted the Friends. After the restoration of

King Charles II in 1660, the Government was particularly afraid of them. At a time of many plots against the King, the Government feared that the Quakers at their silent meetings were plotting the downfall of the state. These suspicions were increased by the fact that Quakers refused to swear – even in a court of law – saying that Christ had forbidden His followers to swear. Because of this, Quakers refused to swear the Oath of Allegiance to the King. In consequence, the Government passed the Quaker Act against them in 1662. And a long period of persecution followed.

The Quakers believe that all men are equal in the eyes of God. In the early days, in order to abolish the distinctions between the social classes, they wore plain clothes and used simple greetings, addressing everyone, be he servant, child or king, with the homely 'thee' and 'thou'.

To this day, Quakers believe that each man should worship God according to his conscience and that no one has a right to use violence against his fellow man. For this reason, Quakers are tolerant of other Christians' beliefs and they will not fight in wars.

Chapter One

They had come to the top of the last hill.

'You can see London,' said Mr Elmy over his shoulder to Rachel and Will.

They scrambled excitedly to their feet. They had both been lying among the vegetables in the back of the bumpy cart – half asleep.

'Is that really London?' exclaimed Rachel, gazing in astonishment at the city spread out on either side of the River Thames.

London did not look at all as she had expected it to look. It was beautiful. Seen from a distance, its gabled houses, its hundred spires, its palaces and parks seemed to shimmer and blur in the stifling August heat. It looked like a city reflected in water. Its beauty surprised her. For London was cruel. Father had said it was cruel. The very reason that they were going there showed how cruel it was.

'Look at all the ships in the River!' shouted Will, jumping up and down in the cart. 'And look at that great bridge!'

He could not conceal his excitement and joy.

London was the largest city in the world. Besides, it was where the King lived.

'Dost thou think that we shall see the King, Father?' he asked.

Rachel frowned at her brother and then gave him a sharp jab with her foot. Will was a great fool, at times.

'My son,' replied their father sternly, driving

on without turning his head. 'Thou know'st we go to the prisons. Not to the Court!'

Two days ago, he had taken them into his quiet study at home at Bledlow Green and told them of old Isaac Newby's death and of the hundreds of Quakers lying without trial in King Charles's prisons.

'We must go to them,' Father had said. 'And share our blessings with them in their need.'

Rachel thought, privately, that everything about their home was a blessing. She loved the rolling Chiltern Hills with the tall beech trees standing sentinels along their crests. And she loved the waving grasses in the forty-acre field and the swallows skimming over the farmyard pond. But they could not take such things with them to London. Instead, they had filled the cart with new potatoes, two sacks of flour, two roast sucking pigs, fresh vegetables, the first honeycomb, and a large basket of purple plums. There were eggs, too, and flat crisp loaves of bread.

'Many of the Friends in prison are scant of food,' their father explained.

As they came down the long hill, the great city looked less beautiful than before. Ragged children with fierce eyes ran out to shout at them from tumbledown shacks along the way. And the nearer they drew to the hundred spires, the stronger grew the evil smell from the open drains.

'What a stink!' exclaimed Will, holding his nose.

Now the cobbles began. Everything suddenly started jumping up and down on the floor of the cart.

'Have a care for the eggs,' Father shouted over the iron rattle of the wheels.

They were in a crowded street by now. Carts and carriages thronged the way. Horses' hooves clattered on the stones. Men jostled and swore. Women screamed. And boys, carrying baskets on their heads, yelled: *'Mack'rel. Fresh Mack'rel.'*

'What a noise! What a horrible noise!' thought Rachel, putting her hands to her ears.

Yet, Will beside her was grinning from ear to ear. His eyes were darting this way and that. And he was asking questions and not listening to the answers – just as he did every year at Thame Fair.

From either side of the street ran lanes and alleys so narrow and dark that Rachel could not understand how anyone could bear to live in them. The wooden gables of the houses almost met overhead, shutting out the bright

summer sky, while along the middle of these narrow ways ran gutters of stinking filth.

'Please, dear Lord,' she prayed silently. 'Don't let Isaac Newby's widow live in a place like that.'

For it was with old Susannah Newby that they were to lodge. Father had told them so before they had set out from home.

As they passed a city church, the clock struck five.

'We have time to go straight to Newgate,' Father called back to them. ''Tis best the Friends have the pork before it spoils in this heat.'

Rachel was hot and tired. They had been two whole days on the journey, for Father had driven them across country to visit a Quaker friend living east of the village of Highgate, where they had spent the night. Her head ached; she felt stiff and bruised by the long bumping in the cart; but, worst of all, she was revolted by the sights and smells of this vast and noisy town. She wished they had never come.

They were driving through Smithfield Market, now. And the hundreds of carcases of

beef hanging up in the butchers' booths and the
buzzing flies and the heavy smell of the meat
and of the oil and tallow stored in the warehouses nearby filled her with a loathing that
made her feel sick.

'I hate London. I hate London,' she told
herself over and over again.

From hating the great city, she fell to being
angry with the cause of their coming.

Why were the London Friends so foolish as to
get themselves sent to prison? she wondered
bitterly. Back in quiet Bledlow Green, none of
the Buckinghamshire Friends had been troubled
by the magistrates for many months. So, the
London Friends, she thought, must have been
stubborn or wicked. They must have committed
some crime.

Yet, her father had not blamed them for their
plight.

'It is time that we leave this happy place,'
was all that he had said when they had left
home. 'It is time that we stand by the London
Friends in their hour of suffering.'

Chapter Two

'It's them stiff-necked Quakers you want, is it?' asked the dour gaoler who met them at the prison gate. 'You're late.'

He explained that by day the Quakers had the liberty of the great hall, but that at dusk they were locked up on the common side with the criminals. That was where they were now.

'May we go to them?' asked Father with gentle insistence.

The gaoler looked doubtfully first at Rachel and then at Will.

'There's murderers and highwaymen and all sorts locked up with your friends,' he said slowly, turning to Father.

'This pork may not keep till the morrow.'

The turnkey looked at the roast sucking pigs slung up on their father's shoulders and then at

Will's skep of green vegetables and Rachel's
armfuls of bread.

'Come along, then,' he grumbled, leading
the way along a cavernous corridor. 'But don't

you say I didn't warn you what you'd find.'

Entering the common side at Newgate at the end of a sultry August day was like walking into the mouth of Hell. The stifling air hit one in the face.

Will gasped. His ears were pricking up with surprise. Rachel clenched her hands tight round the bread.

They stood at the entrance of a large, shadowy chamber, thronged with shadowy men and boys, who turned to stare at them, their faces glimmering like sad moons.

'It's the Quakers they want,' shouted the turnkey. 'Where are they?'

'They're at their prayers, yonder,' squeaked a stunted boy, not much taller than Will, pointing to the far end of the room.

The pickpockets and thieves, the forgers and blackmailers, the murderers and highwaymen opened a path through the wretched crowd, and the turnkey led the way with the three of them following behind, carrying the food.

It was as the boy said. The Friends were holding a Meeting. They were sitting in a circle on the dirty rushes strewn about the floor, with one of their number lying in their midst, his head propped up on a folded cloak.

The sick old man lying on the floor was the first to recognise their father.

'Why, it is Thomas Elmy,' he quavered, his drawn face creasing into a smile. 'Thomas Elmy come to us from Bledlow Green.'

Mr Elmy put down his load quickly and knelt by the old man's side and took both his hands in his own. Yet, something in the set of his shoulders told Rachel that her father did not know who the old man was.

The old man must have guessed this, too.

'Am I so altered, dear Thomas, that thou know'st not who I am? Why, I am Richard Stoddart of Banbury.'

He reminded Mr Elmy in his hoarse voice that they had once ridden across Grange Sands together on their way to Swarthmoor Hall to seek advice of Margaret Fell.

'It was six years ago, if I mind right,' he smiled. 'In the spring of 1660, just before Charles Stuart came back to his throne.'

Rachel and Will stood in the centre of the little group with their vegetables and bread, feeling strangely reassured now that they were among Friends.

'Is the harvest good this year at Bledlow Green?' asked a pale young man at Rachel's side.

She nodded her head and smiled.

'What's the matter with my father's old

friend?' asked Will in too loud a whisper. 'Is he dying?'

'We know not, child,' came the grave answer from a gaunt, middle-aged Quaker. 'But we fear for him. He has the gaol-fever.'

Rachel thought that every one of them looked thin and ill.

Then she remembered the food.

'You must be hungry!' she exclaimed. 'Please take the bread. Please cut the pork. Please eat it now. Straightaway.'

While they cut and divided the victuals, she looked round at their poor pinched faces, and ached with remorse. Not one of the Friends looked foolish or stubborn or wicked. They were good people – gentle and kind. They were just like the Friends at home.

'But what have they *done*?' asked Will angrily as they drove away. 'What have they done to be shut up in that horrible place?'

'They are Friends – like ourselves,' replied Father sadly.

'But it's not wrong to be a Friend,' said Rachel.

'No. But the Government forbids us to gather together at our Meetings on First Day.'

'But *why*?' asked Will. 'I don't understand.'

'The King's advisers think that when we sit in silence and pray to the Lord we are really plotting the downfall of the King.'

'But that's not *true*!' they both exclaimed in horror.

'Of course it is not true. We are a peaceable people.'

Mr Elmy was driving up Watling Street. The lanterns were lit at the corners of the streets. He was puzzled. Susannah Newby lived near Moor Fields. He was not sure of his way.

'Is that all they have done?' asked Rachel in a small, unhappy voice. 'Nothing more than gone to Meeting?'

Her father turned to the left towards Moorgate.

'That is all that they have done, my child.'

Chapter Three

Next morning, the First of September, 1666, Mr Elmy and Rachel and Will took the remaining victuals which they had brought up from Bledlow Green to the Friends imprisoned in the Fleet and at Bridewell.

It was a little cooler. A light east wind was blowing up the River Thames, bringing with it a faint smell of the sea.

Mr Elmy looked calm. Will was more serious and seemed suddenly much older. Even Rachel was no longer afraid. They felt strong. They were both beginning to understand what it meant to be a Friend.

It was as well that this was so. For on that Saturday evening, Thomas Elmy drew his children into old Isaac Newby's library.

'Dear hearts,' he said. 'Tomorrow is First Day. Tomorrow we shall bear witness to our

Faith. We shall go to Meeting.'

Rachel drew in her breath.

'And we may be arrested?' asked Will with a slight catch in his voice.

'If the Lord so wills it,' he said, 'the Friends will be arrested.'

Rachel went to bed that night in her stuffy attic bedroom and tried not to think how frightened she was.

She was a Quaker. She must be brave. She must be as brave as old Richard Stoddart. She must be as brave as Father and Will. And yet – she could not bear the thought of being arrested and thrown into a stifling, dirty prison.

Why had they ever come to this cruel place? When could they go home again? When – oh when – could they return to lovely Bledlow Green?

'Wake up! Wake up!' came drifting into her dreams like falling leaves.

She stirred, opening her eyes. She knew that she was in a strange place. She knew that a great grief lay upon her like a heavy cloak; that something terrible lay ahead.

'Wake up! Oh, do wake up!' whispered Will.

From the shadows in the attic, it must be nearly dawn.

'Why?' she almost shouted, sitting bolt upright.

'Sh!' whispered Will hoarsely. 'Don't make

such a noise. I've found a way out on to the roof.'

Rachel suddenly felt very cross.

'What's so wonderful about that?' she snapped.

'Everything's wonderful!' Will said eagerly. 'It's cool up there. A wind's blowing. And one can see St Paul's Cathedral and the Tower and the River and the whole City. It's laid out like a map. It's like looking down on Oxford Vale from Bledlow Ridge.'

But Rachel still felt cross that he had woken her so suddenly. Besides, she had just remembered the cause of the grief. They were going to Meeting.

'And I think there's a fire,' exclaimed Will.

'A fire?'

'There's a lot of smoke near that great bridge.'

'Let's see,' she said, jumping out of bed.

Will led the way through two empty attics and up a short flight of steps. At the top he opened a little door and, in a moment, the two of them were out on the leads in the long summer dawn.

Rachel gasped.

Mrs Newby's house was very tall. They were standing high above the surrounding chimney-pots. To the south-east across Moor Fields and at the far end of the long city wall rose the four turrets of the famous Tower of London. To the

south-west rose the great pile of St Paul's Cathedral masked in scaffolding. Yet, it was not these that held their eyes. It was the red cloud of smoke low over the houses between themselves and London Bridge.

'It's a fire all right,' said Rachel, seeing a tongue of flame shoot high above a gabled house.

At home a fire was an excitement. Will would saddle his pony and ride three miles to stare at a burning rick.

'Oughtn't we to tell Father and Susannah Newby?' he asked.

When Rachel woke the old widow up, she was disappointingly calm.

'By London Bridge, thou say'st?' she asked. 'That's a long way off.'

'But the smoke's all red and full of flames,' exclaimed Rachel.

'Tush, child,' replied Mrs Newby. 'There's a fire in the City every month. Think no more of it. It will burn itself out like all the rest.'

They returned to their roof-top and were in time to see the flames shooting up a church tower.

'Dost thou think such a fire will just die out – with nothing done?' asked Will, staring wide-eyed at the thickening pall of smoke and the soaring flames.

Just then there were shouts in the street

below them and the sound of footsteps running from Moorgate.

'Let's run down to the kitchen,' Will suggested excitedly. 'And see if Martha has news.'

Mrs Newby's old servant was standing at the street door, shouting to someone in the lane.

'St Magnus Church!' she exclaimed. 'Three hundred houses, thou say'st?'

Looking back on that moment later, Rachel always felt horribly ashamed of herself. Three hundred houses! What luck! she had thought. With a fire as big as that, surely Father would not go to Meeting! The fire was a kind of reprieve.

But she soon found that she was wrong.

'Poor people!' exclaimed Father when he heard the news. 'Poor people! Hurry, children! We must be off to Meeting. Perchance the Friends are in trouble from this fire.'

As they set off in haste towards Cripplegate, men were shouting across the streets to one another.

'They say the Bridge is threatened,' cried one.

'Pray God the wind abates,' cried a second.

Yet, here in this western part of the City there was no sign of panic. The fire was over a mile away. The sun was shining. The bells were ringing. Families clad in their Sunday best were going to church.

At Cripplegate, Mr Elmy turned south in the direction of St Paul's.

'Where do we go for the Meeting?' Will asked his father.

'Down by the River,' he replied shortly. 'Near Blackfriars' Wharf.'

As they walked past the towering walls of the great cathedral, they came up with carts travelling west, stacked high with furniture and

mattresses from the threatened houses round London Bridge. And a minute later, they met a troop of soldiers marching east into Watling Street. They were clearly going to help at the scene of the fire.

Rachel looked at their coarse, grim faces.

'They're too busy with the fire to bother to arrest Quakers,' she thought with relief.

And now they walked south down a crooked lane and crossed Thames Street and turned into a narrow alley between tall buildings, where they could see the River sparkling straight ahead. Mr Elmy turned sharply to the right and led them through a dark courtyard. Then, they climbed some wooden steps and entered a large warehouse.

The Friends were already assembled. They were sitting on benches and on sacks of wheat placed in a rough rectangle, so that the worshippers looked inwards, facing one another.

Rachel sat down between her father and Will, put her hands on her lap and tried to compose her thoughts for prayer. But it was no good. She was too excited about the fire. She was too afraid of the soldiers. Father had made it quite clear that they were breaking the law by coming to Meeting; that the soldiers might come and arrest them, insult them, and throw them into prison. She had just seen how brutal the soldiers looked. And she kept listening for the tramp of their boots coming down the alley. She was terribly afraid. She could feel her heart thumping under her bodice.

At her side, Will had given up all attempts to pray. He was looking instead at the strange ripples of light, reflected up from the River outside the window, which were playing over the walls and rafters of the warehouse. Rachel gave him a nudge. And he lowered his head and sighed. From the wharf below came the slapping sound of the tide against the timbers and mooring-posts and the clear ringing tones of men's voices carried across the water. As she listened, she realised that there must be many boats going up and down the River. There were shouts and halloos from the watermen along the wharves. Were people carrying their goods away from the fire by boat, as well?

She closed her eyes and tried to think of the Lord. Then, she opened them again. It was an

odd place for a Meeting, she thought. Very odd.

Then, she shot a quick, covert look at her father. He was sitting wrapt in prayer, quite oblivious of his strange surroundings; forgetful of the fire. She felt ashamed of herself and yet

comforted – both at the same moment. Her father, at least, was not thinking of the soldiers. He was most truly 'waiting upon the Lord'. Looking at him gave her a sudden feeling of courage.

And then she heard a sound that made her heart thump even louder.

A small band of soldiers was marching down Thames Street. She could hear the rhythmic ring of their boots on the cobbles. Would they pass on towards the fire? Or would they stop and enter the alley?

She looked at the Friends sitting in silence in the warehouse. They might all have been deaf. They were deep in prayer.

And then she heard a shouted command. The troops came to a halt. With another command, the ringing boots came down the lane.

Her father took her right hand gently in his and continued to pray. And Rachel, after a moment's thought, took Will's right hand. And the three of them sat there among the City Friends awaiting the arrival of the soldiers.

They heard the sound of quick steps on the wooden stairs and, a moment later, a young officer burst into the warehouse. He looked at the grave assembly seated silently at prayer and let out a coarse laugh.

'Here's a nest of them,' he shouted back

into the courtyard. 'Up, lads, and rout them out.'

Soldiers clattered up the stairs and poured into the warehouse.

Rachel never forgot the next half hour as long as she lived. It was horrible. She could not believe it. It was like something in a terrible dream.

The soldiers shouted abuse at the Friends. One of them knocked a young apprentice over the head with the staff of his pike. Another pulled an old man by his beard.

'Nay,' protested her father angrily. 'If you have come to arrest us, do your work like men. Not like beasts.'

For answer, two of the soldiers rushed at him and pinioned his arms behind his back.

'Father!' shouted Will in horror.

'Rachel, Will,' he replied steadily. 'Carry yourselves bravely. We bear this for our faith.'

One of the soldiers gave him a cuff across the mouth.

Rachel hid her face in her hands. She could not endure it.

'It's the men we want,' shouted the officer. 'You women take your brats and go home.'

Yet not a woman stirred, save a young seamstress, who had taken off her kerchief and was staunching the wound in the apprentice's head.

'Off with them,' shouted the officer.

The soldiers arrested all the men and herded them like cattle outside in Thames Street, making a kind of pen by holding their pikes lengthwise from one to another.

Rachel and Will tried to stand as near their father as they could.

His mouth looked bruised and hurt, yet somehow he managed to smile at them with his eyes.

'Follow us when we are marched away,' he said. 'See whether they take us to Newgate or to the Fleet or to some other prison. Then return quickly to Susannah Newby and tell her how things have fallen out.'

The officer was taking down the names of his prisoners: Seth Ridge; Tom Fellowes; Richard Johnson; Peter Jackson; Thomas Elmy; Abel Strong; Phineas Smee; John Smith.

They sounded such harmless, ordinary names. They looked such innocent men. Rachel felt she might suddenly burst into tears.

A few minutes later, the officer shouted a quick order, and the troop moved off in the direction of Baynard Castle with their father and his seven companions walking in their midst.

Rachel and Will, white-faced and wretched, ran along level with Mr Elmy.

'Will,' he called out to his son, over the heads of the soldiers. 'I have left money in the chest in Isaac Newby's library. Use it, both of you, if you have need.'

They marched up towards Ludgate Hill, past a belfry pealing its bells, past people coming out of a church.

'It's not Newgate,' cried one of the women running along behind, as the soldiers swung east down the hill. 'It'll be the Fleet.'

But it was not the Fleet Prison either.

The officer marched the prisoners over the Fleet Bridge and into Bride Lane.

They were taking them to Bridewell – the last prison that Rachel and Will and their father had visited the day before.

When the great gates of Bridewell closed shut behind their father, Rachel felt as though the sun had been blotted out of the sky. Father was everything to them. He was the light of their lives.

'What shall we do?' asked Will, his voice breaking in an angry sob.

'Do as he said,' she replied numbly.

She hated to leave him there alone with his bruised mouth and with the shame of that terrible march through the City.

'I hate London. I hate it. I hate it,' cried Will, kicking fiercely at the cobbles of Ludgate Hill.

Chapter Four

'Richard Johnson, thou say'st?' exclaimed Mrs Newby in alarm. 'And Tom Fellowes?'

'Those were two of the Friends, weren't they, Will?' said Rachel.

Will nodded his head. He was in a daze. He could think of nothing but his father's imprisonment and the panic scenes in the streets. The smell of the fire was all over the City. Great smoke clouds were darkening the sky.

'The cart!' exclaimed Mrs Newby. 'Will, can'st thou harness thy father's horse?'

Will nodded his head again. Yes, it was something he could do. He could harness old Dapple.

'The wind's changed,' shouted a passer-by in the street outside. ''Tis blowin' up from the River. St Michael's Church is set alight!'

'Will, Rachel, go quickly. Make ready the

cart,' cried Mrs Newby. 'We have not a moment to lose.'

'What would'st thou, Mistress?' asked the bewildered Martha.

'Martha, make thou ready every bed in the house,' came the quick reply. 'The soldiers have taken Richard Johnson and Tom Fellowes with Thomas Elmy to the Bridewell.'

'Who do we go to fetch?' asked Rachel, when at last the three of them were off and old Dapple and the cart were clattering up Moorgate towards Cheapside.

'There's young Lucy Fellowes, great with child, not thirty yards from St Michael's Church,' explained Mrs Newby. 'And there's old Sarah Johnson – both blind and deaf – in her lodgings close by. With Tom and Richard in prison, they're alone. They have no one to help them.'

In Lombard Street they met the flow of carts carrying furniture away from the riverside blaze. Men were shouting in anger, for further up the street two carriages had interlocked their wheels, barring the road.

'Quick, Will, drive up to the left, before it is

too late,' shouted the old widow. 'Now right. Now right.'

Dapple snorted at the darkness of the lane which they had now entered. Rachel wondered whether Mrs Newby had made a mistake, for the way was so narrow that the cart scraped the

walls of the houses on either side. It was hotter now. They must be quite close to the fire. Their eyes smarted, and pale ashes were floating through the air. Ahead, stretched Cannon Street in a smother of smoke.

'Look!' cried Rachel. 'We can never cross the street.'

She was right. The street was choked with

carts and barrows and people carrying tables and chests on their heads.

'Stop here in the lane,' ordered Mrs Newby.

Beside them, opened a little dark and deserted court.

'Tether thy father's horse to that ring,' she said. 'We must go by foot.'

'Is it far?' asked Will.

He hated to leave Dapple alone at such a time and in such a place. The horse was snickering at the smell of the fire.

But Mrs Newby had no thought for the horse.

'Rachel, Will,' she said urgently. 'Listen hard and quick. When we come to Cannon Street, turn left. Fifty yards on, turn left into St Michael's Lane. Will, dost thou understand?'

Will nodded his head. His eyes were streaming with smoke.

'Lucy Fellowes lives at Number Ten. Tell her we have a cart in St Clement's Lane. And bring her here.'

'And what wilt thou do?' asked Rachel of Mrs Newby.

'I'm for Sarah Johnson. She knows me. She will understand.'

As they came into the pall of smoke from the houses burning in Fish Street, they saw what panic awaited them. Women were screaming. Children were crying.

'Keep together,' shouted Mrs Newby, who had just left them for Mrs Johnson. 'Take each other's hands.'

It was well said, for the press of people fighting their way west with barrows piled with goods would have torn them apart had they not clung together.

And now they could see the burning church. Ash and hot embers were blowing in their faces. The billows of smoke made them choke.

'Put thy cloak about thy face,' gasped Will.

They buried their noses in the rough wool of their cloaks and ran on until they came to the head of St Michael's Lane.

Here, a new confusion awaited them. The fire roared up the church steeple. It roared through the houses in Fish Hill. And the inhabitants of the Lane, convinced that their houses would be set alight next, were throwing

their goods out of the windows. Mattresses and coverlets came flying through the air. A pillow landed on Will's head, split open, and covered him with a cloud of feathers.

'Quick,' cried Rachel, tugging him, spluttering, into the doorway of Number Ten.

The door stood open. The lodging was empty.

'What shall we do?' gasped Will. 'Where can she be?'

'Lucy Fellowes. Lucy Fellowes,' shouted Rachel at the top of her voice.

But there was too much screaming and yelling for anyone to hear. The Lane was thronged with people struggling this way and that, some making towards the River and others carrying pots and pans and stools and clothes piled high on their backs north into Cannon Street and to the safety of the City churches that stood distant from the waterfront.

Rachel and Will looked up and down the Lane, not knowing Mrs Fellowes by sight. They were appalled by the horror about them. Everyone was thinking blindly of himself. No one was trying to put out the fire. Under cover of the panic, a thief immediately in front of their eyes snatched at a poor woman's padded quilt and carried it off. The woman screamed. A man pushing a loaded barrow knocked into her and sent her sprawling against a wall.

'There she is!' yelled Rachel, tugging Will after her towards Thames Street. 'It must be her.'

A young woman was struggling bravely towards the River with something far too heavy perched up on her shoulder.

'Why must it be her?' yelled Will.

'Because it's a cradle. Can'st thou not see? It's a baby's cradle.'

Chapter Five

It was wonderful to be back in Mrs Newby's calm, well-ordered house and to watch young Mrs Fellowes and old Mrs Johnson recovering from their ordeal. Yet, now that Rachel had seen the full horror of the fire, she kept thinking anxiously of her father in Bridewell.

Was he safe? How far would those terrible flames spread?

Bridewell was in all their thoughts.

'My husband! My husband!' Lucy Fellowes had kept saying over and over again as they struggled back along Moorgate – Will and the two women and their few poor belongings in the cart and Mrs Newby and Rachel walking by their side.

It was terrible to think of the Friends – and the debtors and vagabonds, too – shut up in a prison at such a time. Shut up. Unable to escape.

'Lucy,' Mrs Newby had said robustly. 'Bridewell is a mile away. Thou know'st it is. Thy husband is in no danger from the fire!'

But what of the wind, Rachel had thought. It had grown stronger. It was blowing a gale. It was an east wind. To the west of London Bridge, the warehouses were full of oil and tallow and hay. If once they were set alight, the whole City would lie at the mercy of the fire.

They must be with their father. They must. They must. They must go to him at once.

Martha had supper ready for the five of them as soon as they returned. And Rachel, full of her urgent longing, looked across the table at her brother, her unspoken thought blazing in her eyes. Will returned her gaze and nodded his head.

'We want to go to Father,' she burst out. 'We want to go at once.'

Mrs Newby would not hear of it. Bridewell was in no danger, she repeated. The trained bands were pulling down the houses in the path of the fire. The fire would be under control in a matter of hours.

Rachel, who had seen the flames leaping across a whole street, was not convinced.

'We want to be with him,' she said angrily, almost in tears.

'No,' said Mrs Newby firmly. 'It is already dusk. The streets are too dangerous. Besides, you are even now too late.'

'Too late?' asked Will. 'Why?'

'Because the great outer gates will be locked by the time you reach Bridewell.'

'The guards might let us in.'

The old widow shook her head. She said that she had visited the prisons often enough in the last few years to know the rules.

'Go to him tomorrow,' she said. 'And take with you the food that Martha and Lucy and I shall prepare for the Friends. That is time enough.'

Time enough! Rachel wanted to stamp her foot in rage. She could not bear to be kept from her father at such a time. She felt trapped by Mrs Newby's unfeeling common-sense.

It was a terrible night for them both.

Rachel and Will did not undress. They sat up on the high roof in a sheltered nook beside a chimney-stack looking south over the City at the burning wharves.

It was an appalling sight.

Long paths of flames roared westward from Pudding Lane almost to Queen Hythe, reddening the smoke clouds streaming overhead and making the ruined towers and spires of seven churches and the shattered chimney-stacks of countless burnt-out houses stand out in silhouette. Between the flaming streets lay great stretches of blackened, smoking waste.

'It's like the end of the world,' whispered Will.

They huddled close together to keep each other warm and dozed fitfully to the soft crooning of the pigeons roosting on the leads just over their heads. The crooning was a strange comfort. It reminded Rachel of home.

Then they woke up again and stared in anguish at the swift progress of the fire.

Worse still awaited them on the morrow.

In the east, another flawless day dawned over Essex and Kent. But in the City itself it was a day that both of them recalled with horror all their lives.

'Look!' exclaimed Rachel to Will as they ran with the basket of food towards St Paul's and Ludgate Hill. 'Just look at the sun!'

It hung in the sky on the far side of the streaming smoke like an angry, red ball. One could stand and stare at it with one's naked eye. The houses all about them and the great cathedral towering ahead stood in a grey gloaming.

'Let's get to Father quickly,' said Will.

This unnatural turning of night into day and of day into night seemed to them both the prelude of some new and unimaginable catastrophe.

Chapter Six

They found their father in his shirt-sleeves, carrying a huge sack of wheat on his back across the great central courtyard of the prison. Behind him walked the other prisoners, each with a sack on his back.

'Father! Father!' they cried, putting down the heavy basket and running to him.

Mr Elmy stepped aside from the moving file of prisoners, set down his load, and took them in his arms.

'Dear hearts. Dear hearts,' he said over and over again.

'Thou art safe!' cried Rachel joyously, burying her face in the harsh wool of his coat.

'And we're safe, too,' shouted Will foolishly.

'Why, son, so I see,' laughed their father, still holding them tightly. 'Naught wrong save the smell of smoke in thy hair.'

'And Lucy Fellowes is safe and Sarah John-son is safe, too,' said Rachel.

And in a gabble of talk they both began to tell him of yesterday's events.

'Nay. Nay,' he interrupted them. 'Let us tell poor Tom and Richard the good news before all else. They have been sore tried in their hearts.'

Hardly had they called out the good tidings to Tom Fellowes and Richard Johnson when a prison warder shouted to Mr Elmy to get back to his task.

Their father shouldered his sack.

'What art thou doing?' asked Will, running along by his side.

'Moving the wheat into a place of safety.'

'Why?'

'The fire has leapt across Queen Hythe.'

'I know.'

'We heard of it as we came along,' said Rachel.

'There are four thousand quarters of the City's wheat stored here at Bridewell,' panted their father. 'We must save it. It'll be safe in the vaults.'

He disappeared down the steps to the cellars. And Rachel and Will looked on as one prisoner after another passed them, each bent almost double under his heavy load. They looked hot and flushed. The air was heavy with smoke from the raging fire not half a mile away to the east. One could hear the fierce crackle and roar of the flames burning up the rafters of the houses.

Yet, for the moment, being near Father had somehow taken the terror out of the fire.

When Mr Elmy emerged from the cellar and was walking back to the storehouse to fetch another sack, Rachel ran by his side.

'What can we do to help?' she asked.

'Hast thou some of my money in thy pocket, Will?'

Will nodded his head.

'Go then, both of you, to the inn in Bride Lane and bring us back ale – four jugs of ale.'

In their absence, some ill news must have found its way into the prison, for Father looked grey and pinched when they returned.

The prisoners were taking a ten-minute rest.

'Rachel, Will,' he said gravely. 'You must

both stay here with me till the fire is abated.'

'Here? With thee?' exclaimed Rachel, a great surge of relief and happiness sweeping over her.

'Why?' asked Will.

'The City is not safe. The people are frightened.'

'The fire – has it come nearer?'

'Very like,' he replied. 'But it is not the fire that is the danger. It is men's fears. They are looking for the cause of the fire.'

He explained to them that no foreigner was safe in the City. Two Frenchmen and a Dutchman had been attacked in the streets.

'They think *they* started the fire?' asked Will.

Mr Elmy nodded his head.

'And if it be not the foreigners – then men think it must be the Roman Catholics or the . . . or the . . .'

'The Quakers!' exclaimed Rachel, her eyes wide with horror. 'They think *we* set the City alight?'

'A Friend has been beaten nearly to death.'

Chapter Seven

And so it came about that Rachel and Will stood at their father's side on the day of London's doom. And, together, they passed through the fire.

All night they lay on the table in the oriel window of the great chamber where Father and his fellow prisoners slung their hammocks to sleep. Rachel and Will drowsed fitfully in the stifling heat, the light from the burning City streaming through the mighty window. It sent huge shadows of the swaying hammocks swinging over the beautiful ceiling. Bridewell had been a king's palace once, so Father said. The great fire raged not a quarter of a mile away. And whenever Rachel awoke and listened to it, she felt fear gripping her inside.

Yet, there was comfort, too, in this strange bedchamber. Comfort in the swaying hammock

shadows. For in one of the hammocks lay Father. He was near them.

They were all three together.

With daybreak, came a terrible summons to be brave.

A prisoner lying in his hammock immediately over the table where Will and Rachel were asleep, suddenly leapt to the ground, ran to the big oriel window, and then yelled in panic fear:

'The fire's leapt the Fleet Ditch! The fire's upon us!'

Rachel and Will awoke to the cry repeated again and again as the sixty prisoners swinging in their hammocks scrambled in terror to the ground and pressed about the windows.

'It's licking up the prison walls,' cried one.

'We must get out. Get out!' screamed another.

The thieves and pickpockets among them were beginning to stampede like frightened bullocks. They were rushing towards the great oaken door.

'Rachel. Will,' shouted Mr Elmy from fifteen

feet away. 'Get under the table till I can come to you.'

All about them they saw stamping, threshing, milling feet.

'They've locked us in! They've locked us in!' yelled a prisoner, frenziedly pushing against the barred door.

'We're trapped! We're trapped – like rats,' howled another.

Suddenly Rachel and Will saw Father's familiar buckled shoes. A moment later he had jumped on top of the table immediately above them.

'Friends, friends,' he shouted over the heads of the seething mob. 'Calm yourselves.'

The tumult began to die down.

'We are in danger from the fire, it is true,' he continued. 'We are also in danger from ourselves. In our fear we may do injury to one another.'

'Let us out!' cried the prisoners, kicking the door.

'Calm yourselves!' thundered Father. 'When the guards learn of the nearness of the fire they will let us out.'

'Fire! Fire! Fire!' yelled the desperate men.

And now, two other men had leapt on to the table beside their father.

'Hold your clatter,' yelled Tom Fellowes at the men by the door. 'Let us listen to hear if they are coming up the great stairway to unlock the door.'

'Do as he says,' shouted Richard Johnson.

The prisoners ceased their kicking and stood and listened. And, in the silence, Rachel and Will slipped out from the table and jumped up beside their father and the Friends.

The whole great palace chamber stood breathless with hope, waiting for the sound of the warders' feet running up the stairs.

Beyond the stout door not a shout came to them. Not a footfall. All was still.

Behind her, on the other side of the oriel window, Rachel could hear the strange sucking of the flames.

The prisoners groaned.

'They've forgotten us. They've left us to die,' wept a wretched young man, beating his forehead with his fists.

Suddenly Will gave a shout.

'The window, Father!' he yelled. 'The window.'

Everyone in the great chamber turned and stared at the palace window.

It was so heavily ornate that there were only fifteen inches between one stone mullion and the next. And, as if this were not enough to prevent escape, the prison authorities had set iron railings outside the projecting window. These railings looked less than a foot apart.

'But, Will,' said his father slowly. 'Grown men cannot escape through that window.'

'But, Father, I think *I* can,' Will blurted out. 'I could ... could go and tell people of the fire.'

Everyone turned to look at the boy.

Will was strong but small for his age.

'But one foot! Only one foot between the outside railings!'

'He can do it!' cried Rachel. 'I know he can.'

She had suddenly remembered Will climbing into the pigeon loft at home. The loft had a little square sliding window at the side. It was unbelievably small, yet Will had wriggled his way through it to sit among the pigeon droppings inside.

'There's a twenty-foot drop to the ground,' said an old Friend doubtfully. He had long been imprisoned in Bridewell.

'There's our hammocks,' suggested another, more hopefully. 'We could tie them together.'

Will had stripped to his shirt and breeches.

'I can do it, Father,' he grinned. 'I'm sure I can.'

Tom Fellowes was already smashing out the panes with his shoe. Richard Johnson was tugging and twisting at the bits of lead. Two vagabonds were ripping up their canvas hammocks and making a rough kind of rope.

With a sudden roar, the flames licking along the roof ridges in Bride Lane spurted upwards into the sky.

'Rachel,' whispered her father. 'If Will can get through that window, then thou can'st, too.'

'Me?' she exclaimed, astonished. 'Dost thou wish that I try?'

Mr Elmy nodded his head.

'It is my wish, child. Thy brother may need thy help.'

Will had already wriggled through the smashed leaded panes and was grasping the iron railings in his hands. Tom Fellowes was paying out the long hammock rope.

The prisoners crowded round.

'If they've run out and left us,' shouted one, 'then go to the guard room. The keys hang on the hooks on the wall.'

Will was red in the face with the effort of twisting and turning himself through the railings. But at last he was through. He grasped the rope. He turned himself round so that he looked straight inwards at Father and Rachel.

'I've done it!' he grinned, slowly sliding down the rope. 'I'll be back.'

His head disappeared.

Now it was Rachel's turn.

She felt sick. She hated heights. She hated so many people looking on.

'Keep thy eyes looking up,' whispered Father, smiling. 'Will waits for thee on the ground.'

'Don't slide down the rope,' said Tom Fellowes. 'It will hurt thy hands. Hold it tight and *climb* down it.'

She was through the smashed leaded panes. She had grasped the railings. A great wave of hot air swept across her face.

'Get thy shoulders through first,' suggested Richard Johnson.

She could see now that the fire had leapt the Lane. The roof of the prison chapel was ablaze.

Bruised and dizzy, she was through the railings. She grasped the rope.

'Dear Lord,' she sobbed as she climbed down to Will.

She had suddenly realised why Father had sent her, too.

'He fears that we shall not find the key! He fears they will all die up there in the great chamber.'

Chapter Eight

The gates of the prison stood wide open. The courtyard was empty.

'They forgot us!' cried Will, hardly believing his eyes. 'They ran away and left us locked up!'

Smoke was now streaming over the roof of the great chamber where Father and the Friends were imprisoned.

'Where's the guard room?' shouted Rachel.

They did not know. They ran into the little lodge by the gate. There was no row of hooks with the keys hanging up.

They tried the store room; they tried one doorway round the court after another. They looked into the burning chapel and into the deserted quarters for the apprentices. Nowhere could they find the keys.

'Guard room. Guard room,' cried Rachel. 'Where can it be?'

They found it at last at the foot of a squat tower. There were three keys still left on the hooks.

'I'm going to take them all,' shouted Will, seizing the keys, and running towards the foot of the great palace stairs.

There was suddenly a hollow roar to the left. The chapel roof had fallen into the chancel.

'Quick!' gasped Rachel, as they raced up the stairs.

The oaken door stood immediately in front of them. They could hear the thundering of fists on its other side.

'Let us out! Let us out!' yelled the desperate prisoners.

Which was the key?

They tried the largest. It would not fit.

'Will?' came their father's voice. 'Is it thee?'

'Yes, Father,' shouted Will, trying the second key.

Their father sounded urgent.

'When thou unlock'st the door, stand aside. Dost thou understand? Both of you stand flat against the wall.'

What did he mean? Rachel wondered.

The second key did not fit. They pushed home the third.

Will started turning it in the lock.

'Stand by the wall, Rachel!' he suddenly shouted in alarm.

The great door burst open and fifty maddened, frightened men hurtled past them down the stairs.

'Dear hearts. Dear hearts,' murmured their father, gathering them in his grasp and hurrying them down into the courtyard.

Behind them followed the Friends.

In the courtyard they saw that the terrible fire raged not only to the east of Bridewell but also to the north.

'We must make for the River,' shouted Tom Fellowes. 'Follow me.'

He led them past St Bridget's Church and turned left into Fleet Street. Then, left he went again, down Water Lane.

At the end stretched the River.

They stood panting on Whitefriars' Steps, while Tom shouted for a boat. The wide River was full of craft. Numberless lighters were

standing off the Temple, not fifty yards up-
stream, waiting to take off the lawyers' furniture
and books.

'Help us. Help us to cross to the other side,'
shouted Tom.

But the watermen grinned and shrugged their shoulders.

The fire was sweeping through the prison they had just left behind.

'Why will they not help us?' asked Rachel.

Tom turned to Mr Elmy in utter wretchedness.

'We'll never get a boat,' he cried. 'We have no money.'

'Yes, we have!' shouted Will, diving into his pocket.

He brought out a small, rusty knife, a dirty handkerchief and a little wooden spinning-top, and a fire-blackened piece of glass that he had picked up in St Michael's Lane on Sunday afternoon.

He's dropped it, thought Rachel in anguish. It must have fallen out of his pocket as he climbed through the window.

'It's here. It must be here,' said Will, going red in the face.

He dived deeper and pulled out a peeled slip of ash stick and half of a last year's walnut shell.

'There it is!' cried Rachel.

Stuck fast in the walnut shell winked one of

King Charles's new golden guineas.

'It's thine, Father. I took it from Isaac Newby's chest!'

Mr Elmy held the guinea high in the air so that it flashed in the lurid light.

'Here's a whole new guinea if thou tak'st the twelve of us across to Southwark,' he shouted to a grim-faced waterman rowing past.

Chapter Nine

They wandered in the Southwark fields, silently at first and empty of spirit, like people who have been ill and lain long at death's door. Then, they bethought them of the Friends who had been confined in Newgate and the Marshalsea and the Fleet.

How had things fared with them?

Mr Elmy and his companions sought out news among the thousands of weary Londoners camping out in the fields.

'Newgate's burnt down,' a beggar told them. 'But the prisoners – they're safe. Marched out under guards – the lot of them.'

It was the same, they soon learned, at the Marshalsea and the Fleet. Not a single one of His Majesty's prisoners, be he highwayman, thief, or Friend, had lost his life as a result of the fire.

They sat down on the poor trampled grass and gave thanks for God's mercy – quietly, with full hearts.

Across the water, the great pile of St Paul's Cathedral flamed upwards into thick, driving clouds of smoke. All along the River front, the City lay in embers.

Rachel stared at the dying City in silent awe.

'And what do we do now, Father?' asked Will in a small, tired voice.

Father had been talking quietly with Tom Fellowes.

'Why, first, Will,' he replied, 'Tom and myself and the other Friends must surrender ourselves to a justice. The fire does not sct us free from the law of the land.'

'Thou mean'st go back to prison?' cried Will in distress.

'But there isn't a prison for you to go to!' exclaimed an astonished apprentice, sitting on the grass close by. 'They're all burnt down!'

'If the justice gives us our freedom,' continued Mr Elmy, smiling, 'then we shall go home to Bledlow Green.'

Home. Home. To Bledlow Green.

Rachel burst into tears.

'And Tom and Lucy will come with us,' she heard her father say.

'Lucy?' she said breathlessly. 'Lucy Fellowes? Are we taking her too?'

Her father nodded his head and smiled again. 'They need a home for the child.'

Rachel's cup of happiness was suddenly full to overflowing. They were leaving this terrible place. They were going home. Home to the blackberries still shining in the hedges. To the sloes and the damson plums. To the mushrooms coming up in the paddock grass.

Home with Father and Will and Lucy and Tom.

Home to the birth of Lucy's child.

Historical Note

THE GREAT FIRE OF LONDON The Great Fire of London was started in the King's bakery in Pudding Lane in the early hours of Sunday, September 2nd, 1666. At first it was thought to be of little consequence and nothing was done to put it out. But a keen east wind scattered the flames and sparks to the surrounding wooden houses crowded in the narrow streets, and soon the warehouses along the river bank, which were stored with the season's hay and corn as well as tallow and oil, were well alight. The fire was now out of man's control and, with the east wind still blowing, the entire City was at its mercy.

In the course of the next three days, over 13,000 private houses were destroyed, 87 parish churches and St Paul's Cathedral, the Guildhall, Newgate, and three of the City gates, as well as 52 halls of the City companies. Over a million pounds' worth of wine, tobacco, sugar and plums was burnt to cinders.

Appalled by such a dreadful disaster, frightened and angry Londoners tried to blame their misfortunes on the nation's enemies, saying that either the French or the Dutch had set fire to the City. Others put the blame on the Quakers or the Roman Catholics. It is certain, however, that none of these people was responsible. The fire was an accident.

More Beaver Books

We hope you have enjoyed this Beaver Book. Here are some of the other titles:

The Tail of the Trinosaur Charles Causley's splendidly funny verse story about a prehistoric beast which comes to England from the Amazon jungle, with illustrations by Jill Gardiner

The Noah's Ark The story of what happens when George's Noah's Ark animals come to life, by Ruth Ainsworth

Snail Tail A charming story about a snail and his friend, an ant, who go off on a journey

Midnight Adventure The exciting story of how Tim and Gerry catch more than they bargain for when they go fishing at midnight; written and illustrated by Raymond Briggs

Read Me a Story A collection of stories and verse for the youngest children, for reading aloud or for the children to read for themselves, edited by Frank Waters

New Beavers are published every month and if you would like the *Beaver Bulletin* – which gives all the details – please send a stamped addressed envelope to:

Beaver Bulletin
The Hamlyn Group
Astronaut House
Feltham
Middlesex TW14 9AR

387399